# The Tale of Avalon

CARAMEL TREE

# Chapter 1

## What to Wear?

"I see you, Adrian!" Blossom sang out.

"Impossible! I'm at the very top!" Adrian shouted back, giving himself away as he peeked out between the leaves.

Blossom saw him at once and jumped up and down, waving at her friend. "Now it's my turn to hide."

Blossom came to Avalon Castle every day with her mother, Mary, who worked at the castle. Because Adrian was the only child living on the castle grounds, he and Blossom had quickly become the best of friends.

After Adrian had jumped down from the tree, Blossom said, "If only this was a tree like those I have heard of in stories. In other places, there are trees that are covered with delicious fruit. The people there are never hungry because the trees provide food for all."

"That sounds magical," Adrian said. "I will ask my parents if we can buy such a tree."

Blossom smiled. "Maybe each family on the island could have a tree of their very own! Then Mother would not have to work so hard to feed me."

But the King did not know where he could find such a tree. And Mary continued to work long days to put food on the table.

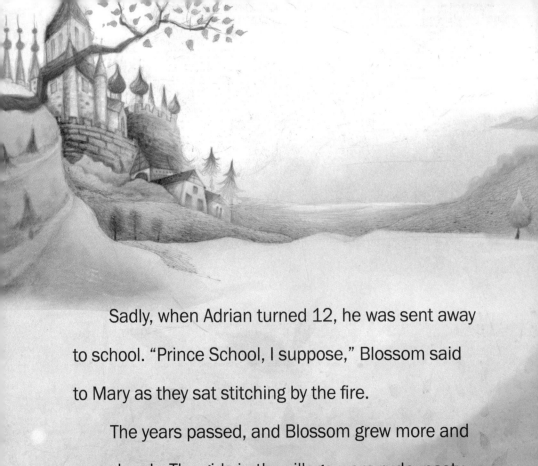

Sadly, when Adrian turned 12, he was sent away to school. "Prince School, I suppose," Blossom said to Mary as they sat stitching by the fire.

The years passed, and Blossom grew more and more lonely. The girls in the village were rude, nasty girls, and shy Blossom liked the company of the woodland animals more than the company of such girls.

When Adrian finished learning to be a prince, he returned to Avalon Castle. The King and Queen decided to throw a spectacular party. They invited everyone on the Island of Avalon.

When the invitation came, Blossom said, "Oh dear, whatever shall I wear?" They looked through her dresses, but it was hopeless. Nothing would do for such a grand event. "That's all right," Blossom said. "It's only a ball, after all."

Her mother's eyes twinkled. "I have just the thing!" She opened the small closet door under the stairs. She pulled out a big sack full of scraps of material she had saved from her work at the castle.

"They're so pretty but so tiny!" Blossom said, picking through the small pieces.

"Never you mind, my child. Off you go while I get to work," her mother said.

"Please, I want to help," Blossom pleaded.

"I want it to be a surprise for you – a beautiful

dress for my beautiful Blossom!" Mary said as she threaded her needle. She closed herself in her room for hours every night. Mary didn't complain, but Blossom could see that her mother's fingers were red and sore from all the extra work.

# Chapter 2

## Luna Spiders

Finally, the gown was ready. "Close your eyes now. No peeking!" Mary said. She hung the dress in front of a window, just as the sun was rising.

When Blossom opened her eyes, she began to cry. The dress shimmered as the pink and gold rays of the rising sun danced through it. "It is surely the most beautiful thing I have ever seen. You are truly a magician!"

She rushed across the room to hug her mother. She stepped carefully into the dress, and Mary fastened the silk buttons up her back. "Of course, you will need slippers," Mary said. She handed Blossom a small pouch.

Inside, Blossom found a pair of soft leather slippers, trimmed with pink and gold satin. "Your grandmother's," Mary said, wiping a tear from her eye. "How she loved to dance!"

The following night, just before sunset, they set off for the castle. Blossom waited outside the kitchen door while Mary delivered some fancy napkins for the ball. As there was no mirror in the cottage, Blossom leaned out over a small pond to see how she looked. All at once, three nasty girls from the village rushed up behind her. They shoved her into the pond and then ran off, laughing like witches.

Blossom sat on a rock, weeping. Her beautiful gown was a mess, and the leather slippers were ruined.

"My dear child!" cried Mary, running to her daughter's side.

Blossom turned to look the other way so her mother would not see her tears. As she turned her head, Blossom noticed a silver spider dangling from a tree branch.

"Oooh!" She jumped up from the rock.

"Hello, Blossom," the spider said.

"I... I... beg your pardon?" Blossom answered.

"I am a Luna spider, Webster." The spider took a small bow.

"Pleased to meet you," Blossom said, curtsying. "But I've never seen a spider with such beautiful clothing." Webster wore a silver suit made from the finest silk.

"Thank you, my dear," he said. "We Luna spiders are a community of tailors. If you wish, I can help you. I can weave a dress of the finest silk for you – a gown that will make you the envy of every other girl at the Prince's ball."

"Oh, Webster! Could you really do that for me?" Blossom asked.

"It would be my pleasure," he answered. "But you must, you MUST, be home before the moon rises. If the Man in the Moon sees you, I cannot be held responsible for what will follow. Do you understand, Blossom?"

She nodded. "I so want to see Adrian again, but not looking like this!" She wrung the water from the hem of her gown.

The tiny spider called his family, and they
went right to work. Blossom and Mary watched in
amazement as the gown and slippers quickly took
shape before their eyes.

When Blossom stepped into the dress, it shimmered as delicately as a spider web dotted with dew in the rosy light of dawn. Webster's wife, Penelope, arranged Blossom's hair, weaving tiny pink blossoms into the strands and sweeping it up on top of her head. Tiny tendrils curled in front of her ears.

"How can we ever thank you?" Mary asked.

"Your happiness is thanks enough for us," Webster answered. "We must go home now, to the moon. But remember – the Man in the Moon must not see you! Luna spiders are only allowed to work at home, on the moon. The Man in the Moon will be very angry if he recognizes our handiwork."

Blossom and Mary hurried into the castle. Adrian was overjoyed to see his childhood friend, and they danced together all night long. After they got over their surprise, the girls from the village sat, sipping pineapple punch, and glaring at the couple.

It was a starless, cloudy night when they finally said goodnight. Mary lit her lantern, and they hurried down the stone steps. Before they were even halfway down, the moon broke out from behind the clouds.

"Run, Blossom! Don't worry about your old mother," Mary cried out. Blossom gathered up her skirts and ran, leaving her mother behind.

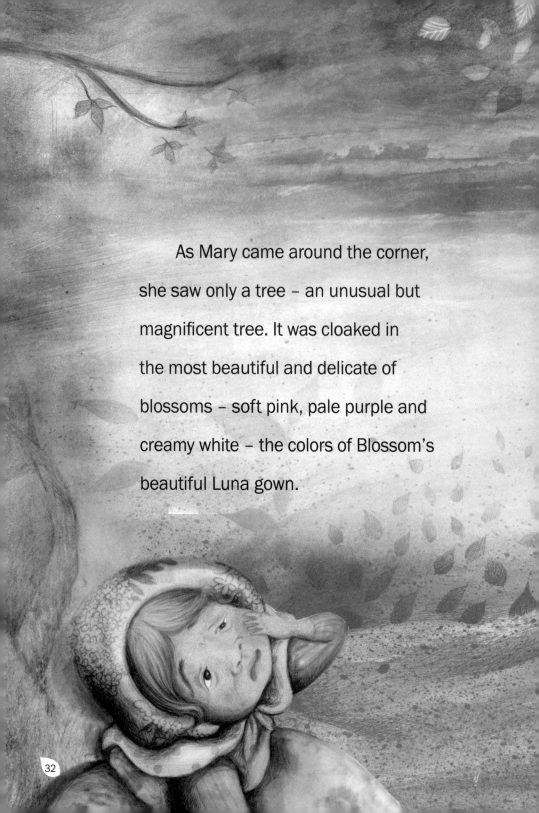

As Mary came around the corner,
she saw only a tree – an unusual but
magnificent tree. It was cloaked in
the most beautiful and delicate of
blossoms – soft pink, pale purple and
creamy white – the colors of Blossom's
beautiful Luna gown.

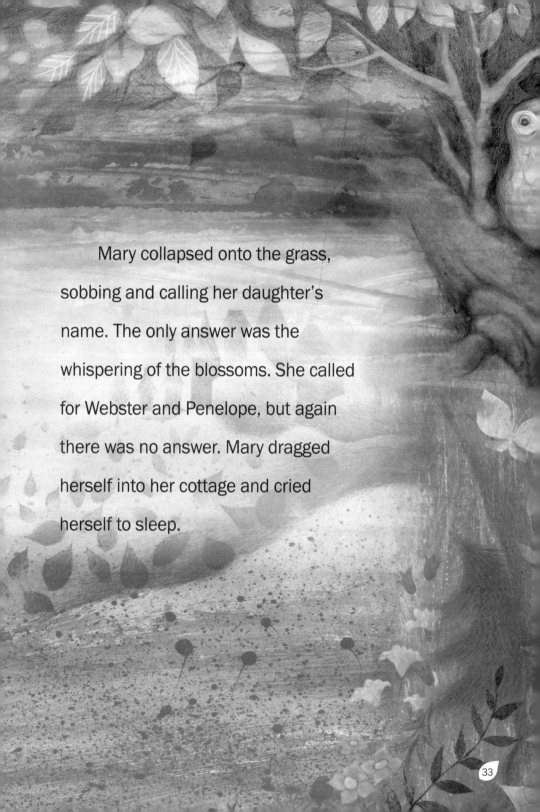

Mary collapsed onto the grass, sobbing and calling her daughter's name. The only answer was the whispering of the blossoms. She called for Webster and Penelope, but again there was no answer. Mary dragged herself into her cottage and cried herself to sleep.

When Adrian came looking for Blossom the next day, Mary said simply that her daughter was gone.

"But why – why would she leave us?" Adrian asked. "Where would she go? How could she leave Avalon?"

Mary shrugged her shoulders. How could she explain to a prince, an educated prince, about a magical Luna spider and the Man in the Moon?

# Chapter 4

## Adrian's Quest

Finally, Adrian turned to go. As he left the cottage, the clouds covered the moon again, and darkness spread across Avalon.

Adrian called out for Blossom as he followed the path until he reached the tree where he had once hidden from his friend. He sank into the grass, leaning back against the tree's rough bark. He began to sob loudly as if his heart were broken, which in fact it was. After a time, he opened his swollen eyes and was shocked to see a spider dangling in front of him. Through his teary eyes, he noticed the spider was very well dressed, especially for a spider.

"Your Highness." Webster bowed low, causing his tiny hat to topple onto Adrian's knee.

"Why... h... h... hello," Adrian replied, picking up the little hat.

"I am a Luna spider," Webster said. "I can help you find your true love, your beautiful Blossom."

The prince got down on his hands and knees, being careful not to disturb the silver strand from which Webster dangled. "I'll do anything. What do you ask of me?" he said.

"Only this," Webster replied. "The tree you see here is truly a magical tree. It can produce fruit far sweeter than anything you have ever tasted."

"Blossom used to long for such a tree," Adrian said.

Webster nodded. "On a night when the moon is full, you must promise to take the seeds from 12 pieces of the fruit and plant them all over the Island of Avalon. As long as you shall live, the people of your kingdom will always have food to eat and enough to share. Do you understand?"

"Of course," Adrian answered. "It will be my pleasure to do as you ask, my wise little friend. But this tree has never produced any fruit at all."

"Please be patient," Webster replied. "Now, you must return tonight when the moon first appears. Stand beside this beautiful tree of blossoms and speak to the Man in the Moon. Tell him the name you have chosen for this wonderful fruit. If he approves, he will return your love to you. If not, she will remain lost forever."

"I understand, but how am I to choose a name?" Adrian asked.

"That I cannot help you with, sir," Webster said. "And now I fear I must be off. Good luck!"

# Chapter 5
## Blossom's Magical Tree

All day long, Adrian walked the fields and paths of Avalon, looking for a sign, something to help him choose the right name for the fruit.

As the sun was setting, he found himself back at the door of Mary's cottage. Adrian told her of his visit with Webster and she nodded; she knew exactly of whom he spoke. As Adrian explained his quest, her eyes lit up.

"My great grandfather told stories of an ancient tree that once bore such magical fruit!" she exclaimed, rubbing her forehead. "Oh, my memory is so poor. Now whatever did he call that fruit? Attle? No... Appen? No... Aha! Apple! That is it! The fruit was named *apple*, and he described it just as Webster described this fruit to you. He said the apple was the sweetest food in all the world."

Adrian hugged Mary and hurried outside to wait by the tree. The perfume of the blossoms reminded him of his own sweet Blossom, and he looked eagerly at the sky for a glimpse of the moon.

Alas, it was a night full of clouds and darkness. Thunder rumbled in the distance, and a flash of lightning lit up the sky. Adrian waited impatiently and finally drifted off to sleep, leaning back against the rough bark of the tree. Suddenly, he jerked awake as a loud voice boomed forth from the sky.

"WELL?" it said.

Adrian jumped to his feet. "Oh, thank you, Mr. Moon. I... I... I... think I have found the perfect name for the fruit of this most marvelous tree."

"AND?" the Man in the Moon replied.